The Wager

DARK-HUNTERS: LORDS OF AVALON

Sherrilyn Kenyon

Nemesis Publications
Franklin, TN

LORDS OF AVALON

LordsOfAvalon.com

COPYRIGHT © 1985, 2002, 2006, 2017 SHERRILYN MCQUEEN

Mighty Barnacle, LLC
PO BOX 67
Thompson's Station, TN/37179
www.mightybarnacle.com

Ordering Information:
MYKENYON.COM

THE WAGER / SHERRILYN MCQUEEN —3rd ed.
ISBN-10: 0-9994530-0-9
ISBN-13: 978-0-9994530-0-1

For everyone who believes in magick...

*90% of intelligence is knowing
when to shut the $%ck up!*

—Malene M. Woodward

Hell Hath No Fury . . .

I t'd been a long, cold...

Millennium.

Thomas paused as he penned those words. Surely it wasn't that long. Was it? Frowning, he looked at the calendar on his PDA that Merlin had brought to him from what future man would call the twenty-first century, and gave a low whistle.

It hadn't been quite that long, even though he lived in a land where time had no real meaning. It only felt like it, and therefore he left the word on the paper. It sounded better than saying just a few centuries—and that was what writing was all about he'd learned. The truth was important, but not so much as keeping his audience entertained. News bored people, but stories...

That was where the money was. At least for people other than him. There was no money here, nor much of anything else.

But he was digressing. Millennium or not, it had been way too long since he'd last been free.

He who bargains with the devil pays with eternity. His dear old mangled mother had been fond of the saying. Too bad he hadn't been better at listening—but then that was the problem with "conversation." So many times even when you paused for a breath, you weren't really listening to the other person so much as planning your next speech. Of course, he'd been a cocky youth.

What did some old crone know about anything, anyway? he used to think. He was Thomas Malory. *Sir* Thomas Malory—couldn't forget the Sir part. That was all important.

In his day that Sir had meant that he was a man with standing. A man with prospects.

A man with no friggin' clue (Thom really liked the vernacular Percival had taught him from other centuries. There was just such color to some of the later phraseology... but now to return to what he'd been thinking).

Life had begun easy enough for him. He'd been born into a well-to-do family. A *nice* family... Nice incidentally was a four lettered word. Look it up, it really was. It meant to be agreeable. Pleasant. Courteous.

Boring.

Like any good youth worth his salt, he'd run as far away from nice as he could. Nice was for the weak (another four lettered word). It was for a doddering fool (see how everything vile led back to four letters {even vile was four letters}).

And Thomas was anything but a fool.

Or so he'd thought.

Until the day he'd met *her* (Please insert footnote here that in French, *la douleur* i.e. pain was feminine). There was a reason for that. Women, not money, were the root of all evil (it was a trick of their gender that woman was five and not four letters, but then girl was four letters, too. This was done to throw poor men off so that we wouldn't realize just how corrupt and detrimental they were). Of course, there should be some warning, given the fact that it was woe-man. And they were ever a woe to any man.

But back to the point of our story. Women were the root of all evil. No doubt. Or at the very least the fall of every good man.

And Thom should know. He'd been doing quite well for himself until that fateful day when *she* had shown herself to him. Like a vision of heaven, she'd been crossing the street wearing a gown of blue. Or maybe it was green. Hell, after all these centuries it could have been brown. The color hadn't mattered at the time because in truth he'd been picturing her naked in his mind.

And he'd learned one very important lesson. Never picture a woman naked when she was capable of reading your mind. At least not unless you were seriously into masochism.

Thom wasn't. Then again, given his current predicament, perhaps he was.

Only a true masochist would dart across the street to meet and fall in love with Merlin.

Thom paused in his writing. "Now, good reader, before you think me odd. Let me explain. You see Merlin in ancient Britain wasn't a name. It was a title and the one who bore that title could be either male or female. And my Merlin was a beautiful blond angel who just happens to be a little less than forgiving. How do I know? See first paragraph where I talk about being imprisoned for a millennium.... give or take a few centuries which still doesn't sound quite as impressive as millennium."

Thom felt a little better after uttering that speech. Though not much. How could any man feel better while stuck in a hole?

For it was true. Hell had no fury greater than a woman's wrath.

Or scorn.

Nay, wrath.

"That's what having a beer with your buddies will get you."

Well, in his case it was more like a keg of ale. But that would be jumping ahead of the story.

Sighing at himself, Thom dipped his quill in ink and returned to his vellum sheet. It was true, he had other means of writing things down, but since it all began with a quill and vellum, he wanted this diatribe to be captured the same way. After all, this was his version of the story. Or more simply, this was the truth of the matter. While others only speculated, he knew it for what it really was.

And no, the truth would not set him free. Only Merlin could do that and well, that was an entirely different story from this one.

This story began with a poor besotted man seeing his Aphrodite across the street. She had paused in her walk and was looking about as if she'd lost something.

Me, he'd thought. *You have lost me and I am right here.*

With no thought except to hear the sound of his beloved's voice before she started on her way again, he'd headed toward her only to nearly die under the hooves of a horse as Thom stepped out in front of a carter. Thom not so deftly dodged the carter and landed extremely unceremoniously in a trough.

Drenched, but still besotted by Cupid's whim, Thom attempted to wring himself dry before he again headed toward her... this time a bit more cautious of traffic.

He couldn't breathe. Couldn't think.

Couldn't dry the damn stench of the reeking water off his clothes. All he could do was watch his Calypso as she waited (he told himself) for him to claim her.

As he drew near her, a million clever thoughts and introductions popped eagerly into his mind. He was going to sweep her off her feet with witty repartee. She would be bedazzled by his nimble, elegant tongue (in more ways than one if everything went according to plan).

And then she had looked at him. Those brilliant blue... or maybe they were green, eyes had pierced him with curiosity.

Thom had drawn a deep breath, opened his mouth to speak to woo her with his charm when all of a sudden his cleverness abandoned him.

Nothing. His mind was blank.

Worthless. Aggravating.

"Greetings." Even he cringed as that simple, stupid word had tumbled out of his lips.

"Greetings, good sir."

Her voice had been clear and soft. Like the song of an angel. She'd stood there for a moment, looking expectantly at him while his heart pounded, his forehead beaded with sweat.

And still nothing clever came to mind. In fact, nothing at all was there.

Speak, Thom, speak.

"Nice day, eh?"

"Very nice."

Aye, he was a fool. One who no longer bore any trace of his shriveled manhood. Wanting to save whatever dignity he possessed (which at this point was in the negative digits), Thom nodded. "I just thought I'd point it out to you, fair maiden. Good day."

Cringing even more, he'd started away from her only to pause as he caught sight of something strange.

Now being a rational human being, he'd thought it an unusually large bird. Let's face it, in fifteenth century England, everyone spoke of dragons, but no one had really thought to ever see one.

And yet there it was in the sky... Like a giant...

Dragon. Which it was. Large and black with big red bulbous eyes and gleaming scales, it had circled above them, blocking out the sun.

Thomas being a coward had wanted to run, but being a lusty man, he quickly saw an opportunity to woo his fair lady with dashing actions and not a feeble tongue. After all, what woman wouldn't swoon over a dragonslayer?

That had been the idea.

At least until the dragon kicked his ass. With one swipe of a talon, the dragon had batted him into the building. Thom had fallen to the street and every part of his body had throbbed and ached.

It was awful. Or so he'd thought until the woman had placed her hand on his forehead. One minute he'd been lying on the street, reeking of trough water, and in the next he'd found himself lying on a large, gilded bed.

"Where am I?"

"Shh," his angel had said. "You have been poisoned by the dragon. Lie still and give my touch time to heal you or you will surely die."

(*Note to self. I should have started moving about, thrashing wildly*).

Not wanting to die (because I was stupid), Thom had done as she asked. He had lain there, looking up into her perfectly sculpted features. She was beauty and grace incarnate.

"Have you a name, my lady?"

"Merlin."

That had been the last name he would have ever attributed to a woman so comely. "Merlin?"

"Aye. Now be still."

For the first time in all of his life, Thom had obeyed. He'd closed his eyes and inhaled the fresh, sweet scent of lilac that clung to the bed he lay in. He'd wondered if this was Merlin's bed and then he'd pondered of other things that men and women could do in a bed... especially together.

"Stop that."

He opened his eyes at the reprimand from his Aphrodite. "Stop what?"

"Those thoughts," she'd said sharply. "I hear every one of them and they disturb me."

"Disturb you how?"

"I am the Penmerlin and I must remain chaste. Thoughts such as those do not belong in my head."

"They're not in your head, my lady, they're in mine, and if they offend you, perhaps you should keep to yourself."

She'd gifted him with a dazzling smile. "You are a bold one, Thom. Perhaps I should have let the mandrake take you."

"Mandrake?" As in the root?

"The dragon," she'd explained. "His kind have the ability to take either the form of man or dragon, hence their name."

Well that certainly explained that, however other matters had been rather vague in his mind. "But he wasn't after me. He was after you. Why?"

"Because I was on the trail of a very special Merlin and the mandrake sensed me. That is why I so seldom venture to the world of man. When one possesses as much magick as I do, it is too easy for other magical beasts to find you."

That made sense to him. "You are enemies."

She nodded. "He works for Morgen le Fey."

Thom'd had the audacity to laugh at that. "The sister of King Arthur."

Merlin hadn't joined in his laughter. "Aye, the very same."

The serious look on her face and the tone of her voice had instantly sobered him. "You're not japing."

"Nay. The tales of Arthur are real, but they are not quite what the minstrels tell. Arthur's world was vast and his battles are still being waged, not only in this time, but in future ones as well."

In that moment, Thom wasn't sure what enraptured him most. The stunning creature he longed to bed or the idea that Camelot really had existed.

Over the course of the next few days while he healed from his attack, Thom had stayed in the fabled isle of Avalon and listened to Merlin's stories of Arthur and his knights.

But more than that, he'd seen them. At least those who still lived. There for a week, he'd walked amongst the legends and shook the hands of fables. He'd learned that Merlin was only one of her kind. Others like her had been sent out into the world of mortal man to be hidden from Morgen who wanted to use those Merlins and the sacred objects they protected for evil.

It was a frightening battle they waged. One that held no regard for time or beings. And in the end, the very fate of the world rested in the hands of the victor.

"I wish to be one of you," Thom had finally confessed to Merlin on the evening of his eighth day. "I want to help save the world."

Her eyes had turned dull. "That isn't your destiny, Thom. You must return to the world of man and be as you were."

She made that sound so simple enough, but he wasn't the same man who had come to Avalon. His time here had changed him. "How can I ever be as I was, now that I know the truth?"

She'd stepped away from him. "You will be as you were, Thom... I promise."

And then everything had gone blurry. His eyesight had failed until he'd found himself encased in darkness.

Thom awakened the next morning to find himself back in England, in his own house... his own bed.

He'd tried desperately to return to Avalon, only to have everyone tell him that'd he'd dreamed it all.

"You've been here the whole time," his housekeeper had sworn.

But he hadn't believed it. How could he? This wasn't some illness that had befallen him. It wasn't.

It'd been real (another four letter word that often led men to disaster).

Eventually, Thom had convinced himself that they were right and he'd dreamed it all. The land of Merlins had only existed in his mind. Where else could it have been?

And so he'd returned to his old ways. He'd gambled, he'd fought, he'd wenched, and most of all he'd drunk and drunk and drunk.

Until *that* night.

It was a night (another noun that was five letters in English and four in French. There were times when the French were greatly astute). Thom had wandered off to his favorite tavern that was filled with many of his less than proper friends.

As the night passed, and they'd fallen deep into their cups, Geoffrey, or maybe it'd been Henry or Richard, had begun to place a wager.

He who told the best tale would win a purse of coin (again, note the four letters here).

No one knew how much coin was in the purse because they were all too drunk to care. Instead, they had begun with their stories before a small group of wenches who were their judges.

Thom, too drunk to notice that a man had drawn near their table, had fondled his wench while the others went on before him.

"That's all well and nice," he'd said as Richard finished up some retelling of one of Chaucer's tales (the man was far from original). "But I, Thomas Malory... *Sir* Thomas Malory can beat you all."

"Of course you can, Thom," Geoffrey had said with a laugh and a belch. "You always *think* you can."

"Nay, nay, there is no think... I'm too drunk for that. This is all about doing." He'd held his cup out to be refilled before he'd started the story. At first he'd meant to tell the story of a farming mishap his father had told him of, but before he could think better of it (drinking usually had this effect on most), out had come the whole matter of the King Arthur Merlin had told him about.

Or at least some of it. Being Thom who liked to embellish all truth, he'd taken some liberties. He'd changed a few things, but basically he'd kept to the story. After all, what harm could come of it? He'd dreamed it all anyway, and it was an interesting tale.

And the next thing he'd known, he'd won that wager and taken home a purse—which later proved to only contain two rocks and some lint. A paltry prize indeed.

Then, before he'd even known what had happened, people had starting coming up to him and speaking of a book he'd written. Thom, not being a fool to let such fame bypass him, had played along at first. Until he'd seen the book himself. There it was, in all beautiful glory.

His name.

No man had ever destroyed his life more quickly than Thom did the moment that book became commonly available.

One instant he'd been in his own bed, and the next he'd been in a small, tiny, infinitesimal cell with an angry blond angel glaring at him.

"Do I know you?" he'd asked her.

She'd glared at him. Out of nowhere, *the* book had appeared. "How could you do this?"

Now at this time, self-preservation had caused Thom to ask the one question that had been getting men into trouble for centuries. "Do what?"

And just like countless men before him (and after him, is this not true, men?) he'd learned too late that he should have remained completely silent.

"You have unleashed our secret, Thomas. Doom to you for it, because with this book you have exposed us to those who want us dead."

Suddenly, his dream returned to him and he remembered every bit of it. Most of all, he remembered that it wasn't a dream.

The Lords of Avalon were all real... just as Morgen was. And as Merlin led the remnants of the Knights of the Round Table, Morgen led her Circle of the Damned. Two halves fighting for the world.

But that left Thom with just one question. "If you had all that magick, Merlin? Why didn't you know about the book that would be written if you returned me to the world?"

With those words uttered, he'd learned that there truly was a worse question to ask a woman than A) her age, B) her weight and C) do what?

"Please note that here I rot and here I stay until Merlin cools down."

Thom looked down at the PDA and sighed. Time might not have any real meaning in Avalon, but it meant a whole hell of a lot to him. And at the rate it was ticking by, Merlin would never let him go.

BROGAN

CONCEPT SKETCH
FOR MERLIN

DABEL BROTHERS
CONCEPT SKETCH
FOR MERLIN & KERRIGAN

CONCEPT SKETCH
FOR MERLIN & KERRIGAN

Don't miss these fun titles!

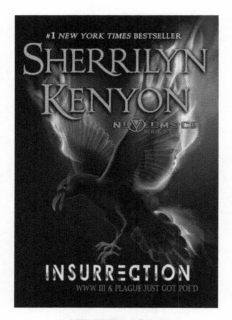
The virus ran swiftly on the hot summer breeze.

Unseen. Unheard. Unknown.

It swept through the entire earth in a matter of months, having mercy on no one. Young—old—it didn't matter.

Brought to us by the Drabs, it was the last thing we expected. But the Drabs knew. They even fought a war over whether or not they should save us.

In the end, it was decided that we were diseased insects who were unfit to breathe their air.

Our air.

So they left the human race to die a miserable death of agonizing pain. Left us with no doctors or medicine. Their plan was to rid the earth of us and to take our home as their own.

What they never expected was the change that would come after the plague. We didn't all die as they'd planned. Those under the age of twenty somehow managed to survive the disease.

We managed to pull through it, even alone, and we learned to hide ourselves while our bodies changed. Still human, but now something else. Something more powerful. More intuitive.

More pissed off.

We're still here, on this earth, and we're not leaving. This is *our* home.

Our planet.

Drabs take note and learn to be afraid. You've had a hundred years here on earth, but now your time here is done.

You called us rodents. Insects. Diseased animals. The scraps of humanity—and *that*, my Drab friend, we certainly are. But what you should have realized is that you can't kill a Scrap. Humanity isn't dead. Not by a longshot. We still have our soldiers and we have our conviction.

Most of all, we have hope.

And we will win in the end. Whatever it takes. Whatever it costs. We won't allow you to take our planet from us. So count your days, Drabs.

The war is on.

Chapter 1

"Well that little hissy fit is certainly going to get their attention. So much for keeping a low profile, huh? You might as well have just set fire to your nuts on the Capitol lawn."

Leaning back in his chair, Josiah hated to admit just how right Anjelica Shepherd might be. Except for one thing . . . "This didn't leave me sterile."

"No, but if they catch you—" she gestured at his crotch—"They're going straight for your no-zone, buddy. Trust me, those little friends of yours will be the first thing they take and fry up for a main course."

He flashed a grin at her. "Then let's make sure they don't, shall we?"

She rolled her dark brown eyes at him. And shook her head so forcefully, it made the beads in her Nubian braids jingle. "Don't even go there, Old Man Crow."

He ignored her play on his last name of *Crow* and the fact that he was half Apsáalooke.

Anjelica was one of the few who knew that little tidbit about him—along with the major secret he kept as sacred as a vestal virgin matron in charge of her convent's vault of chastity belt keys.

Just as he was the only one who knew she and her daughter, Kyisha, had made their way from the refugee camps out of Louisiana to the hills of Tennessee where they were currently in hiding.

And she was lucky. He killed most people who knew anything about him. A necessity he'd learned a long time ago.

Keep your secrets close and you live longer. Keep your enemies dead and you live longer still.

But that was neither here nor there.

"I didn't start this war, Anj." The Drabs had, a hundred years ago when they'd brought their disease to the earth and left the human race to die out in utter misery.

Had left him an orphaned mutant with skills that defied everyone's expectations. Even his own.

Yeah, you should have made sure I stayed dead.

Their mistake.

Shakespeare had once written that hell hath no fury like a woman scorned. He was wrong. Hell hath no fury like a human forced to watch everything he or she loved be ripped away while the one who did it stood back and gloated in selfish, smug satisfaction.

Male. Female. Made no never mind.

If the history of humanity had any lesson to be learned whatsoever it should have been that no one fought harder than the home team. Whether it was the Athenians at Marathon, the Battle of Stirling Bridge, the Spartan Three Hundred, Alfred the Great, the Colonial Americans, or even the Native Americans who'd kicked Eric the Red's ass out of Vinland—humans were capable of overcoming unimaginable odds and superior technology and tactics whenever they were protecting their own.

No one got the better of them. It was never about the size of the dog in the fight, but all about the size of the bite in the dog.

Too bad the Drabs had burned all human literature and history books instead of reading some.

Now they were about to get schooled at the University of Serious Bell Ringing by Dr. Crow and his elite faculty of kick-your-ass-and-make-it-count.

Because Josiah had no intention of stopping until he hand-delivered the bill that was long past due, and shoved it down their gray, Drab throats and made them choke on it.

This was personal. They had made it so.

His gaze fell to the latest report that had prompted his declaration of war. And his throat tightened around the bile that rose up in angry indignation. "Did you hear? They burned Phoenix last night."

Anjelica winced. "I saw the footage. Did anyone escape?"

He forced himself to mask the kick-in-the-gut he felt over her question. "If they did, they haven't surfaced yet. No doubt they're in hiding. Afraid of being caught."

"Yeah. I'd dig in deep, too. And pray hard for the hand of death to pass me by." She jerked her chin toward his secured laptop that he'd used to post his message on the Drab's network. "That the real reason for your declaration of war tonight?"

He nodded even as disgust, fear and hopelessness threatened to overwhelm him. The human race couldn't afford such strikes against them. It'd taken a hundred years of hiding from the Drab tracesakers who'd been assigned to hunt them down, to rebuild their underground population back from the near-extinction levels that had almost wiped them off the planet.

Another hit like this and they might become history, after all.

"My little tantrum should get the heat off the survivors. . . . If there are any. The tracesakers will start looking for me now." It was what the Drabs always did whenever they sensed a threat.

Any action required a swift and direct overreaction.

Anjelica tsked at him. "Boy, you're insane. You done bought yourself all kinds of hurt."

"Perhaps, but remember what William Blake said. *The eagle never lost so much time, as when he submitted to learn of the crow.* If I can buy them even an hour of peace, I will give up my life for it."

He meant that. Yet he had no intention of dying. Not to today.

Not tomorrow.

Not ever.

He was, after all, a crow. And crows were sacred to his people. They were messengers and harbingers. A gateway from this world to the next.

As his mother used to say . . .

One crow caws for sorrow.

Two crows sing of joy.

Three crows fly to borrow.

Four crows are a ploy.

Five crows warn of tomorrow.

Six crows bring much gold.

And seven crows caution you of all the stories left untold.

Josiah had been the seventh crow born in his family. His mother's youngest.

Her deadliest and most unpredictable.

I swear, Joey, you came into this world backwards and you've been that way ever since. Cantankerous and stubborn as the day is long. Ain't no one ever been born what could tell you what to do.

But then that, too, ran deep in his blood. Deeper still in his people and his family.

Again, the Drabs should have learned something of the culture they sought to destroy. It was easy to hate without context. To destroy without understanding how difficult it was to build something.

Unlike them, he'd taken his time to carefully study his enemies. Intimately. He knew how they thought. How they lived and how they'd developed into their current collective mind-set.

Now he was going to use that to destroy them.

Once and for all.

Starting with the one who'd delivered the deepest blow to his heart.

Without a word, his gaze fell to the poem he'd written just before his declaration. This particular bit of his writing, he would forever keep to himself.

A silent promise. Just between the two of them.

Her name he didn't speak. He didn't have to.

She knew who she was.

He knew who she was. That was all that mattered.

And he would have her throat. Come hell or high water. Come nuclear devastation. Even if he had to fight his way back from death again.

Josiah would bathe in her blood and he would feast on her heart. After all, that was where his middle name had come from. His mother's original maiden name.

*All*red.

Given to their ancestor who'd been known for coating himself in the blood of his slain enemies and reveling in the violence of war. Her entire family had been peace-loving until crossed. Then it was on to such an extent that his father used to joke their unwritten family motto was: *I'll kill you.*

And Josiah wouldn't rest until he saw this through . . .

Tick tock rang the clock. The talons of death came nearer nigh.

In the dark, all was stark. And only your breath was heard as a wretched sigh.

On the wall, the shadows fall. As you ran the entire hallway's span.

Yet with every step, you continually wept. For you knew the end would be coming soon.

No matter how hard you tried, or deep you cried, still you felt your impending doom.

You felt it there, beneath the stair, or lurking in the shadowed pane.

And still you tried. Still you vied. Ever seeking to grow your infernal fame.

All the while, you lived in denial. Knowing for you there'd be no reprieve.

Not for ye who always deceived.

Coward, liar, thief and whore.

May you get all you deserve and more.

To hell I hope you will soon be bound.

And never again will ye be found.

May your name forever be stricken from each and every tongue.

And may never again let any praise for you be sung.

For you have spread poison and lies upon this land.

And you deserve nothing save utter misery and deepest reprimand.

In time I hope you come to wear,

All the shame you once dispensed with giddy flare.

For this to the heavens I do so decree.

And know in my heart that so will it be.

"From me to you, bitch. From me to you."

They *are among us.*

Daria Stazen shivered at the electronic signs being broadcast all around their school. Images flickered on the walls and lockers, showing all the shapes and sizes and disguises those creatures could take and how they could easily blend in without anyone ever knowing.

It was such a chilling thought that one of her classmates could be one to *them* in hiding.

A human being.

She shuddered in revulsion and fear. Then glanced about suspiciously at everyone in her hallway. How would she ever know?

Could it be the strange girl on her right whose gray skin was a shade darker than the others? Or the boy to her left whose skin was a tiny bit bluer? Or the teacher whose lips held more black to them? Or what about the custodian whose black eyes had pupils that didn't seem to dilate properly? He said it came from an accident in his youth.

But what if it wasn't?

What if he were a human using some kind of magic or drug to disguise his real features? The documentaries all warned that humans were extremely cunning.

Highly dangerous.

"Are you all right?"

She almost screamed as Tamira came up behind her to speak in her ear. "Don't do that!"

"Do what?" she asked innocently.

"Sneak up on me when I'm scaring myself with really creepy thoughts about humans being here!" Daria waved her hand in front of her unit to open it automatically and pull out her sweater and gear for gym. Like her, Tamira was slightly taller than average and rather muscular, with pale gray skin and dark ebony eyes and hair. They were both from warrior caste families, but Daria's father had been granted a special dispensation to attend university after he'd scored exceptionally high on his entrance tests in upper primary.

Now he was one of their top rated scientists— like her mother. Daria was hoping to follow in their footsteps. If she could stop being late to her classes all the time . . .

She closed her unit and paused as she caught Tamira staring at the images, too.

They were mesmerizing. As all good nightmares tended to be.

Tamira jerked her chin at the human they showed transforming himself into the unerring image of a Materian, right down to the dual noble birthmarks Daria had been fortunate enough to inherit in perfect symmetry at the edges of her mouth. It was something all of her friends envied her for.

"You think we'll ever see a real human?"

Daria clutched at her designer bag that her father had brought to her all the way from their homeworld on his last trip there. "Hope not."

Tamira arched her brow at that. "Why? Aren't you curious about them?"

Not even a little. "They're disease-ridden, for one thing."

She laughed. "Oh please! How can you say that? We're the ones who brought it to them. Besides, it was a simple cold."

"Exactly! They were so weak a species, the sniffles killed them off. How can you admire a race that can't even survive a mere head cold?"

Tamira scoffed. "You are so cynical. No wonder they chose you for the committee."

Lifting her chin proudly, Daria patted her badge that proclaimed her chairwoman of HELL—Human Extermination Licensing Leaders. It was now officially her job to help investigate and find any humans who might infiltrate their school or youth community. "Yes, well, the humans are a threat we need to eradicate."

"Why? You just said they were so weak as to be ridiculous."

Daria growled in frustration of her friend's continued churlishness. Sometimes she swore Tamira would argue with a sign post! "That doesn't mean they couldn't mutate it into something worse. Like bird flu and wipe us out with it!" That was, after all, what their people had fought a civil war over when they'd first landed on this planet a hundred years ago.

Rodents and humans. Same thing. Parasites could do all kinds of damage to higher organisms.

Basic biology.

Why any Materian had ever thought a single human would be worth saving, she couldn't imagine. Everything she'd read said they were a barbaric lot who'd been on the brink of war with each other all the time back then. No culture. No higher tech. They'd never done anything particularly noteworthy as a race.

Mass extinction had been the greatest kindness for them.

Not that it mattered. They were gone and the Materians were here now. This was their planet and it would remain so. It'd been theirs since the last of the major human cities had succumbed to the final wave of plagues and her people had burned the last of the human bodies and shed the planet of their feeble disease-ridden remnants.

All that was left now were bits and pieces that only the most daring Materians collected as curiosities.

"Hey Day!"

She paused as she heard Frayne's deep voice. Her heart quickened.

Tamira's eyes darkened with jealousy an instant before she caught herself. As did most of the girls in the hallway. But then Daria was used to that. Frayne was one of the most eligible boys in their city. The son of their territorial regent, he would one day rise to a seat of political power to rival or surpass his mother's. And because she was a third cousin to their ruling family, he had his eye on her.

Daria liked to pretend he had other interests in her as well, but she wasn't completely stupid. If she were someone else, he might still talk to her and date her from time to time.

But . . .

He pressed his cheek to hers and took her bag. "Did you not get my message?"

"What message?"

He tsked. "My mother's been called out of town tonight." He wagged his eyebrows at her. "Want to come over and study some biology? Up close and personal?"

She snorted at his less than subtle innuendo. "Nice. I'm surprised you didn't announce it over the intercom."

"Want me to? I will!"

"No, thank you. I don't have anywhere to hide your body and prison doesn't look good on my university applications."

He laughed. "But it would give you a leg up for the military."

"Possibly." Daria sobered as she glanced over his shoulder and caught the strange expression on Xared's face as he stared at her badge. "Something wrong?"

A full head taller than Frayne and even more ripped and better looking, there were a number of people who speculated that Xared was the more accomplished athlete, but because of Frayne's social status, Xared pulled back in matches and let Frayne take the best shots to win. Some claimed he did the same on tests, too, making sure he always took second place to Frayne, in all things.

She wasn't so sure about that, but right now there was something strange going on. She could feel it deep in her bones. And since she'd known Xared since birth, they were more akin to family than friends. In fact, he was the closest thing to a sibling she'd ever known.

"Hadn't heard about your promotion. Congrats."

Yet the chilly undertone of his voice didn't match those words.

At all.

Something was bothering him and she didn't like to be the cause of his strife.

"Thanks. I think. Although, I'm feeling a little frostbite."

He blinked and offered up a half-hearted smile. "Sorry. I was hoping I'd get it. Last I heard it was mine, so I was a little shocked to see you with the badge."

Oh, *that* explained it. And it made her feel even worse that she'd deprived him of anything. Unlike Frayne, she didn't take joy in beating others out of their dreams. "I had no idea, Xed! I'm so sorry. If you want, I'll decline it for you and you can take my place."

He held his hand up. "It's fine. Really. They obviously wanted you for it, and I am happy for you to have it. It just shocked me, but I'm over it now." The warmth returned to his eyes. "Couldn't imagine it going to a better, Materian. Peace to my sister." He clutched his hand to his heart in a symbol of eternal kinship.

She duplicated the gesture. "Peace to my brother. Always. You know I love you."

"Love you, too." He clapped Frayne on his arm. "I'm headed on to class. Roundabout!"

"Roundabout!" they said in parting.

As they headed the opposite way, Frayne handed her a small silver charm. The unexpected gift delighted her. However, there was one tiny problem. "Thank you! But . . . what is it?"

"I found it in the bathroom. It's a human symbol."

Her stomach shrank. "What?!"

Nodding, he jerked his chin in the direction Xed had gone. "Xed dropped it from his bag. I had to look it up to find out what it was."

"And what is it?"

"An ankie or something like that. The humans use it to identify each other and sympathizers to their cause."

Suddenly, she felt sick with fear and dread. "What are saying?"

"That either Xed is a human being in disguise or he's in league their cause. Whichever it is, you have to report him. It's your job."

She shook her head in horror. "He's like brother to me!"

"And you swore an oath. Loyalty above everything."

Daria wanted to weep at his dire tone and the cruel light in his dark eyes. One that was mirrored by Tamira's. Worse was the unspoken threat that hovered in the air between them.

If she didn't report Xed and see him arrested, the two of them would report them both.

Every Crow Has Its Murder

MY KENYON
READ IT. LOVE IT.

Visit us online. SherrilynKenyon.com

ABOUT THE AUTHOR

New York Times and international bestselling author, Sherrilyn Kenyon, is a regular at the #1 spot. With legions of fans known as Menyons (thousands of whom proudly sport tattoos from her series and who travel from all over the world to attend her appearances), her books are always snatched up as soon as they appear on store shelves. Since 2003, she had placed more than 80 novels on the New York Times list in all formats including manga and graphic novels. Current series are: Dark-Hunter®, Chronicles of Nick®, Deadman's Cross™, Nevermore™, Silent Swans™, Lords of Avalon® and The League®. Her books are available in over 100 countries where eager fans impatiently wait for the next release. The Chronicles of Nick® and Dark-Hunter® series are soon to be major motion pictures while Dark-Hunter®, Lords of Avalon® and The League® are being developed for television. Join her and her Menyons online at SherrilynKenyon.com

CPSIA information can be obtained
at www.ICGtesting.com
Printed in the USA
LVHW021357020820
662080LV00006B/616